CLEVELAND RADIO PLAYERS

Published by Cleveland Radio Players

Copyright © 2015 by Milton Matthew Horowitz

All rights, including the right of reproduction in whole or in part, in any form, including digital reproduction, are reserved. Published in the United States by Cleveland Radio Players.

CAUTION: Professionals and amateurs are hereby warned that *The Jolly Frogger*, being fully protected under the Copyright Laws of the United States is subject to royalty. All rights, including professional, amateur, motion picture, recitation, lecturing, public reading, radio and television broadcasting, and the rights of translation into foreign languages, are strictly reserved. Particular emphasis is laid on the question of readings, permission for which must be secured in writing from the author's representative at Cleveland Radio Players, 2218 Superior Ave, Suite 203, Cleveland, OH 44114. The amateur acting rights of *The Jolly Frogger* are controlled exclusively for the author by the author's representative.

ISBN **978-0692462874** (Cleveland Radio Players, The)

Original Adaption and Performances

Originally adapted for the radio and performed
by The Cleveland Radio Players. Directed by
Milton Matthew Horowitz. Recorded at Bad Racket
Studios.

Starring:
(in order of appearance)

Beau Reinker	Captain Gray Beard
Kat Bi	Bar Wench
Charles Hargrave	One-Eyed Jack
Cat Kenney	Toothy
Ned Kalafat	Drunk Pete
Eric Sever	Silk Pants

Pirate Gang

Llenelle Gibson
Deanna Dionne
David Flynt
Michael Lawrence
Jack Hunt

The Jolly Frogger

By

Jack Matuszewski

Adapted By
Milton Matthew Horowitz

© The Cleveland Radio Players theradioplayers@gmail.com

for rights and royalties   2218 Superior Ave, Suite #203
please visit: Cleveland Ohio 44114
clevelandradioplayers.com
                                216 269 4171

THE TALE OF THE JOLLY FROGGER

CAST OF CHARACTERS

Capetian Gray Beard

Bar Wench

Jack

Toothy

Pete

Silk-Pants

Pirate 1, 2, 3

Pirate X, Y, Z

OPENING CREDITS

> THE VOICE OF THE CLEVELAND RADIO PLAYERS
> Hello... This is the voice of The
> Cleveland Radio Players... My name
> is Denny Castiglione, ladies and
> gentlemen,

> OPENING FANFARE
> and you're listening to The
> Cleveland Radio Players performance
> of THE JOLLY FROGGER. Written by
> Jack Matuszewski. Directed by
> Milton Matthew Horowitz. Narrated
> by XXXX

ACT 1

SCENE 1 PIRATE TAVERN

> FADE IN TAVERN SFX
> FADE IN TAVERN MUSIC

> PIRATE GANG
> What shall we do with a drunken
> sailor? What shall we do with a
> drunken sailor? What shall we do
> with a drunken sailor,

> PIRATE LEADER
> Err-eye-lee in the mornin'

PIRATE GANG
Throw him in th' bilge and make him
drink it, Throw him in th' bilge
and make him drink it, Throw him in
th' bilge and make him drink it,

PIRATE LEADER
Err-eye-lee in the mornin'.

PIRATE GANG
Shave his belly with a rusty razor,
Shave his belly with a rusty razor,
Shave his belly with a rusty razor,

PIRATE LEADER
Err-eye-lee in the mornin'...

PIRATE GANG
Put 'em in the bed with the
Captain's daughter, Put 'em in the
bed with the Captain's daughter,
Put 'em in the bed with the
Captain's daughter,

PIRATE LEADER
Err-eye-lee in the mornin'... Ah
hahahaha

ALL PIRATES LAUGH

(beat)

FOOTSTEPS
DRINK ON TABLE

DRINK POUR

BAR WENCH
Aww, c'mon now, Cap'n Gray Beard
...Why ain't 'cha singin' with the
rest of 'em... Not like you to be
drinking by yerself...

CAPTAIN GRAY BEARD
Ah, it's just... The singin'... It
reminds me of me old first mate...
God bless his soul.

BAR WENCH
Oh, I'm sorry Captain... How did he
die?

CAPTAIN GRAY BEARD
I don't know...? I'm not even sure
he did?

                    BAR WENCH
Oh. Well, usually when a pirate
says that, it's because somebody
died...

                    CAPTAIN GRAY BEARD
Aye... That might be so...

                    BAR WENCH
Well, if you don't know how he
died, or even if he is dead, then
why are you so sad?

                    CAPTAIN GRAY BEARD
Well, I s'pose I'm so sad because
when I last seen him I was being
thrown overboard me own ship in a
treacherous mutiny plot from a
bunch of unfaithful crewmen the sea
wouldn't even swallow.

                    BAR WENCH
Jeez... Sounds like ya cheated
death Cap'n. You should feel lucky
to have escaped with your life...

                    CAPTAIN GRAY BEARD
Don'tcha think I do? Not a day goes
by I don't think about them boys...
and what what I'd do to 'em if'n I
ever did lay eyes on 'em again...
But they're probably dead now...

                    BAR WENCH
What do ya think happened to 'em?

                    CAPTAIN GRAY BEARD
Well, I only know what happened to
'em up to a point... Ya see, once I
was thrown overboard, I quickly
lost sight of me ol' ship... I was
lost at sea for two days before I
floated upon a discarded whiskey
barrel I rode to this deserted
island...

                    BAR WENCH
What makes you think they're all
dead?

                    CAPTAIN GRAY BEARD
Me ol' first mate... I tried to
warn 'em all but they didn't

                    CAPTAIN GRAY BEARD
listen... WHY DIDN'T THEY BELIEVE
ME!!! Oh ho ho... It's no hope...

                         CAPTAIN GRAY BEARD SOBS

          BAR WENCH
I don't understand. I thought you
were mutinied off your ship... How
do you know they're dead?

          CAPTAIN GRAY BEARD
Because my ol' first mate is a
ruthless killer, and I know he
probably killed most of 'em, if not
all of 'em, before they did him in
too... Boo hooo hooo hoo..

                    CAPTAIN GRAY BEARD SOBS MORE

          BAR WENCH
Look I don't usually ask sobbing
mutinied Captains to tell me
long-winded pirate stories, but you
look like you really need someone
to talk to...

          CAPTAIN GRAY BEARD
Oh I, don't mean to be a bother...
I couldn't.

          BAR WENCH
Well ok--

          CAPTAIN GRAY BEARD
Alright! I'll tell ya me story
already...!

          BAR WENCH
Uh huh...

          CAPTAIN GRAY BEARD
Just pour me another one of them
drinks...

               GLASS ON TABLE
               POURING WHISKEY
                         CAPTAIN GRAY BEARD DRINKS

          CAPTAIN GRAY BEARD
Okay... This par-tick-ular story
takes place on an extremely
stereotypical pirate ship with some

                    CAPTAIN GRAY BEARD
extremely stereotypical pirates on
board.

                              FADE OUT ENVIRONMENT

                    CAPTAIN GRAY BEARD
Now let me see here... The begining
of the story would be... Uh...
Well... Wait, how did this story
start again... Oh yeah, that's
right...

SCENE 2 THE DECK OF THE JOLLY FROGGER

                                   MUSKET FIRE

                    DYING PIRATE
Gaahhhhhh....

                    CAPTAIN GRAY BEARD
          (v.o.)
Yeah, I had just shot a scallywag
for not cleanin' after me sea
bird...

               FADE IN OPEN SEA SFX
                         FADE IN PIRATE SHIP AMBIANCE

                    CAPTAIN GRAY BEARD
          (v.o.)
I remember standing with a pistol
in my hand over the dead body of
another pirate... And I looked at
the rest of me crew and I says...

                    CAPTAIN GRAY BEARD
All right then, ya scurvy dogs, let
that be a lesson to all of ya...
The next time any one of ya's
fer-gets to clean out me parrot's
cage you'll get ten times worse
than this sorry sod did. Now dump
this poor pile o'bones into the
drink.

               FOOTSTEPS ON WOOD DECK X2
                    DRAGGING BODY
                    DRAGGING CHAINS

                              BODY SPLASH

                    CAPTAIN GRAY BEARD
Now then, because me old first
matey was, slackin' with his parrot
duties, I'll be needin' to assign a
new one, and I've got just the man
in mind. He's a lad who's been with
me through many a hard time,
traveled with me all over the
world, and witnessed some of the
most beautiful and gruesome pirate
atrocities ever imaginable with me.

                                    SHORT FOOTSTEPS

                    JACK
Ah Gray Beard y'ol' softy, you.
you've no need to be goin' on, for
I know that it MUST be me you're
talking 'bout. I mean, who else
besides me, one-eyed Jack, has been
with ya through the most gruesome
of times? Why, I was there when we
two got a wee bit grogged up and
you seduced that fair maiden with
the head of a snake and the body of
a red hot spike!

                            HEARTY PATS ON THE BACK

                    CAPTAIN GRAY BEARD
Ah Jack, I be meanin' no disrespect
to ya, we did have good times...
and every time I feel a red hot
spike on me skin I think of ya. But
I'm afraid in these matters yer a
bit mistaken.

                    JACK SNEERS
            SHORT FOOTSTEPS ON WOOD
                            PIRATE GANG WHISPERS

                    CAPTAIN GRAY BEARD
Naw. The man I be speakin' about is
a fearless cutthroat who cares so
much 'bout sheddin' blood that
he'll shed as much of his own as he
has to just so that he can keep on
harmin' the innocent.

                            FOOTSTEPS WITH LIMP

                    TOOTHY
Arr, never were there truer words
spoken 'bout yer dear chum Toothy.
Fer if ever there were a dog who'd
sacrifice anything to keep on
spillin' blood it was me! Why you
Gray Beard can even testify to that
yourself. Fer I remember a day long
ago when we two were cornered by
five of the king's imperial
guardsmen. We had two pistols on
hand but unfortunately we had
'emptied all our rounds while
huntin' fer possums earlier that
day. With five able-bodied men
bearin' down on us and no
ammunition in sight, you'll recall
that I pulled out five of me own
teeth and loaded them to our guns
so that we might survive.

              CAPTAIN GRAY BEARD
And survive we did indeed, Toothy,
but methinks ye had better quit
your reminicin' while yer ahead.
Fer even tho I hate to disappoint
ya, I speak of yet another damned
pirate soul.

          FOOTSTEPS WITH LIMP AWAY

                        PIRATE GANG JEERS

              CAPTAIN GRAY BEARD
As horrid as the two o'you are, I
know that you're nothing in regards
to yer grog, and me new first mate
HAS to be a man who enjoys his
grog--

              DRUNKEN FOOTSTEPS

                    CORK AND BOTTLE SWIG

                    DRUNK PETE
               (drunk and slurring)
Awe Cap'n... This is great... Not
only am I the youngest of the
pirates... And the best looking...
But now you're gonna be makin' me
your first mate? That's really
sweeet... Come 'ere, lemme put my
arm around ya!

            BOTTLE SWIG AND SPLASH

                        DRUNK PETE LAUGH

Why I'm so happy, Cap'n, I could
kiss ya...!

                    DRUNK PETE KISSES AT CAPTAIN

            CAPTAIN GRAY BEARD
PEEEET!!... Yer a drunken...
Stinkin'... LOUT!... And I love
ya!!

            DRUNK PETE
Aww thanks, Cap'm.

            CAPTAIN GRAY BEARD
But any man who'd make you his
first matey would have to be
cracked in the head.

            DRUNK PETE
Awwwww...

                  STUMBLING STEPS ON WOOD AWAY

            CAPTAIN GRAY BEARD
Besides, me new man can out-drink
the lot o'ye... Inebriated Pete
included.

                    PIRATES JEER AND GASP

            CAPTAIN GRAY BEARD
That's right! Me new first mate is
a man more vicious than Toothy,
more gruesome than one-eyed Jack,
and even more of a drunkard than
Inebriated Pete!

                  PIRATES JEER INQUISITIVLY

            TOOTHY
Well for the lov'o God, man, don't
keep us waitin'!

            JACK
Aye! If such a man exists, bring
'im out here and show us!

            DRUNK PETE
YEAH!!

                  STUMBLING AND FALLING THUD

ALL PIRATES
(ad-lib) Yeah- Show him- Bring his
oily hide out here- Let's see 'im
in the flesh!

CAPTAIN GRAY BEARD
(yelling) ALL RIGHT ALL RIGHT!!
Quit yer belly-achin', me lads! May
I introduce to you the most evil
pirate of 'em all. The Dreaded
Pirate... Silk-Pants!

TAP DANCE LIKE FOOTSTEPS

SILK-PANTS
Well hey there, mateys!

CAPTAIN GRAY BEARD
What did I tell yeh, men! The most
fearsome pirate ye's ever did set
eyes upon. Ye can see now why
sailors tremble and women swoon at
the sight of the Dreaded Pirate
Silk-Pants! Ain't that right, men?

PIRATES JEER CONFUSED
I, said... (Yelling) Ain't that
RIGHT, men!?

JACK
Uhhh... Cap'n, don't ya think yer
makin' a bit of a mistake? I mean,
look, Cap'n... He's wearing pink
and silver.

TOOTHY
Yeah... And what's with that silly
feather stickin' out of his hat?...
You guys see that?

CAPTAIN GRAY BEARD
Whatever do ya mean thar, laddie?

PETE
(Blurting out) He's sure as hell
don't look like a very tough pirate
none, Cap'n!

PIRATES JEER

TOOTHY
I agree with Pete for once Cap'n...
That sorry son of a woman ain't
much of a man at'all!

SILK-PANTS

Hey!

CAPTAIN GRAY BEARD

Now that'll be enough out o' all of
ya! This here Silk-Pants is worth
more than his weight in feathers!
Silk-Pants will make a great first
mate, and as such:

SWORD DRAWN FROM SHEATH

I, Wingleslash Haptiback Greybeard
the fourth... Captain of the Gray
Bailer, hereby proclaim the Dreaded
Pirate Silk-Pants as its official
first mate!... Now, I'll have no
more of this here rabble-rousin' or
I'll consider it a form of mutiny
and have the lot of ya flogged!

JACK

Come on now, Cap'n, ya can't be
serious in makin' him your first
mate... I mean, what kind of a
pirate name is "Silk-Pants" anyway?

SILK-PANTS

Well, ya know, when I became a
pirate I knew I had to get
juuuuussst the right name that
would suit me. So naturally I went
through all the normal pirate
names: Turquoise Beard, Octavio the
Fierce, Three-Legged Geoffrey,
Asian Gary... but I just really
couldn't feel any of those; they
weren't ME. So I took some time to
think it over, ya know, drank some
hot tea did some yoga-- and then I
just knew, it was just there... it
hit me like a bolt of lightning.
What was totally me? What fits me
better than even my name does?
Silk. Pants. So it was settled-- I
am... The Dreaded Pirate
Silk-Pants!

CAPTAIN GRAY BEARD

(Enthusiastically) Ya see?! That be
a touchin' pirate story if I ever
did hear one. Silk-pants may be a
true terror on the high seas, but
he's also a man of compassion and
sensitivity!

                    PETE
Aww, does he HAVE to be the first
mate?

                    GRAY
YES! And in addition to
commenceratin' him as me first mate
I also have an announcement to
make... NO longer will be the same
old plunder and pillage
opportunists... Silk-Pants has
brought to my attention that these
practices are a little out of date
with today's modern pirates... And
we need to be on the cutting edge
of innovation when it comes to
pirating... And no longer does
plundering spread the word of this
here ship in a way that does it
justice... So from now on instead
of being stereotypical
pirate-types, we're going to set
out on a new adventure that will
reap 10 times the gold we use to
make...

                    PIRATES JEER IN AGREEMENT
And will spread our name across
every sea...

                    PIRATES JEER ENTHUSIASTICALLY
WHAT I'M TALKING ABOUT IS FROG
LEGS, BOYS!

                              SILENT PAUSE

                    DRUNK PETE
WHAT?

                    CAPTAIN GRAY BEARD
That's right, men... From now on
we're gonna be wranglin' frogs and
sailin' to the Orient to sell 'em
so as they can make 'em into frog
legs for supper.

                    TOOTHY
Frogs?! You can't be serious,
Captain? How's the name of our
ship, The Gray Bailer, gonna sound
fishing for frogs near the main
land?

PIRATES JEER NEGATIVELY

                    JACK
Yeah! The Gray Bailer is known for
its terror on the high sea...

                    CAPTAIN GRAY BEARD
That's another thing I be meanin'
to talk to ya's about... Ya see, on
account of us changing our mode-iss
operand-iss We'll be changin' the
name of the ship too... From now
on, we will be known as the Jolly
Frogger...

                    TOOTHY
The what?!

                              PIRATES JEER NEGATIVELY

                    CAPTAIN GRAY BEARD
The Jolly Frogger... That's
right... Based on me new first
mate's vast knowledge of trade
routes, he's assured me that the
frogleg trading market is an
overlooked opportunity for us to
make some serious gold.

                    SILK-PANTS
And it helps promote alternative
meats...

                              PIRATES JEER NEGATIVELY

                    JACK
You're seriously gonna change the
name of the ship?! But The Gray
Bailer is a well-known and feared
ship we pirates take great pride
in...

                    CAPTAIN GRAY BEARD
That's right! We have some new
ideas we think you'll be even more
proud of... The Silk-Pants has also
told me that the froglegs are very
popular in some countries and even
used as an, uh, afra-dee-gee-ak in
some places.

                              PIRATES JEER CONFUSED

                    SILK-PANTS
That's so true... Frogleg soup
allllways put 'em in the mood...

                    CAPTAIN GRAY BEARD
We also have a few ideas about
making this here crew a bit more
fun and entertaining to be a part
of, so as to gain more pirates in
numbers when we visit the
mainlands... And I think ya'll be
joyfully impressed with some of the
new changes that we'll be
implementin' on this here ship...
THE JOLLY FROGGER... and I don't
wanna hear no guff about it! In
fact, we're gonna be doing some
more group activities to strengthen
company moralle around here.

                    SILK-PANTS
Seriously, you guys... These new
changes are like gonna make you
merrier then a mermaid in the sea.

                    CAPTAIN GRAY BEARD
Ya see, men... That's a true pirate
thinkin' about his crew's happiness
first, and always ahead of the rest
of 'em... Right men? ...I said,
RIGHT MEN?!

                    ALL PIRATES
Aye Aye... Captain...

                    CAPTAIN GRAY BEARD
Now, you guys get the ship in shape
while the Silk-Pants and I finish
out the new plans... Now come along
then, Silk-Pants, we've got some
plannin' ta do. I need ya to help
me plot a new course. We're settin'
sail for our next course to the
bountifully frog-rich shores near
the Foja Mountains of Indonesia!

                    SILK-PANTS
(again singing) AYE AAYYEE
CAP'N!... Exit... Port-side...

                    CAPTAIN GRAY BEARD
And as fer the rest a yahs... Get
back ta work!

FOOTSTEPS ON WOOD

TAP DANCE AWAY SFX

                    CAPTAIN GRAY BEARD
                         (v.o.)
Now the thing you need to
understand 'bout the Silk-Pants,
is... He... Sails to his own breeze
as they say... Ya know, what I
means to say is, he's from a place
where they do things differently...
And by differently, I mean with a
lot more spirit and spunk than your
typical swashbuckler... And my
crew, well, they weren't so quick
to adapt to the Silk-Pants new
routine... And by routine, I mean
dance routine... That's right,
everyday high noon the First Mate
Silk-Pants would lead the crew of
the Jolly Frogger in a song and
dance number...

SCENE 3 THE DECK OF THE JOLLY FROGER DAYS LATER

                              FADE IN SHIP ENVIRONMENT

                    CAPTAIN GRAY BEARD
I sure hope you're right about this
here musical song and dance routine
ya got the crew learnin'.
Regardless ... It sure is
entertaining...

                    SILK-PANTS
Trust me... When they get a load of
this little number in Sri-Lanka,
word will spread like froglegs
across the Orient of our gay little
ship... OKAY matey's lets take it
again from the top... And a one,
and a two, and a one, two, three,
four...

                              CUE MUSICAL MUSIC

        (singing and clapping)
A Yan-kee ship came down the
riv-er...

                              TAP DANCE SOUNDS

                    ALL PIRATES
Blow, boys, blow!

                    SILK-PANTS
Her masts and spars they shone like
silver!

                    ALL PIRATES
Blow, my bully boys, blow!

                    SILK-PANTS
How do you know she's a Yankee
liner?

                    ALL PIRATES
Blow, boys, blow!

                    SILK-PANTS
The stars and stripes float out
behind her!

                    ALL PIRATES
Blow, my bully boys, blow!

                    SILK-PANTS
How do you know she's a Yankee
packet?

                    ALL PIRATES
Blow, boys, blow!

                    SILK-PANTS
They fired a gun, I heard the
racket!

                    ALL PIRATES
Blow, my bully boys, blow!...

                    SILK-PANTS
No... no, NO!

                         PIRATES JEER NEGATIVELY
Toothy! You are ALL off-key and
you're forgetting to smile... And
Jack, I know you only have one good
eye, but you HAVE to see that you
are WAY off-tempo with your
footwork... And Pete... Well, good
job, I was very impressed you
didn't fall down that time... Look,
we're gonna take a 5-minute break,
pirates, and then were gonna try
this again, mmm'kay?

TIP TAP STEPS AWAY

                TOOTHY
Are you guys kidding me? How much
longer are we gonna put up with
this?

                JACK
Agreed!... I was definitely on
tempo. It was Pete! He keeps
screwin' up the tempo!

                PETE
It was not!... It was Toothy who's
got the crazy legs!

                    PIRATES ARGUE ROBUSTLY

                CAPTAIN GRAY BEARD
            (v.o.)
Now, what I didn't know was that
when Silk-Pants and I left the crew
to their duties... They began to
let their natural paranoia get the
best of them... Stir crazy, they
call it... They started plottin' a
mutiny against the Silk-Pants and
I...

SCENE 4 THE CREW BEGINS TO PLOT

                    PACING FOOTSTEPS ON WOOD

                TOOTHY
All right then, ya dogs! I think we
can all agree that this an outrage!

                    PIRATES CHEER

                PETE
YEAH!... The food here is
TERRIBLE!!

                JACK
Not that ya idgit! We're talking
'bout the Silk-Pants!

                PETE
Oh. Yeah!

                TOOTHY
We three have been faithful crewmen
ta tha Cap'n fer years, and what

                    TOOTHY
does he do? He goes and hires some
silken princess fer his first mate!

                    JACK
That's right. All of us have seen
him through thick and thin. We've
been his closest compatriots all
his pirate life. Why, Toothy,
weren't you the one who pulled his
sorry arse outta the drink while he
was bein' attacked by that vicious
gang o' seals? And as fer me!?
Well, I think you can all recall
that I was the one who helped him
and this entire crew escape from
the dreaded French dungeons armed
with nothin' but a wooden spoon and
me left shoe!

                    PETE
Yeah... And that one time I gave
him the last doughnut!... And he
didn't even say THANK YOU!

                    TOOTHY
So I think it's understood that
something has to be done here.

                              PIRATES JEER IN AGREEMENT

                    TOOTHY
We can't be sittin' around tak'n
orders from, from that there,
daff-ee-dill!

                    JACK
But what can we do, Toothy?

                    TOOTHY
I'll tell ya what we're gonna do!
We're gonna bring the Cap'n out
here and demand that he make ME,
Toothy, the REAL first mate!... Or
else!

                    PETE
Or else what?

                    TOOTHY
Or else... We'll tie him up
and... And deal with him
AH-CORD-ING-LY... And I think y'all
know what that means!

PIRATES LAUGH SINISTERLY

(beat)

                    PETE
Yeah!... We could steal their
boots!

                              STOP LAUGHING

                    TOOTHY
Before we can do anything, we'll
have to get the agreement of the
whole crew before we set the fires
o' mutiny burnin'... ALL AGREED?

                    ALL PIRATES
AYE!

                         EVIL PIRATE LAUGHTER

                    TOOTHY
Inebriated Pete! You and the rest
o' the crew go below deck and make
the arrangements while I soliloquy
here on the deck sinisterly...

                    PETE AND JACK
Aye, aye, Toothy.

          FOOTSTEPS RUNNING ON WOOD X2
                         EMOTIONAL MUSIC SWELL

                    TOOTHY
Too long have I sailed upon this
rickety pile 'o driftwood with
nothing to call me own... It's true
I've known Cap'n Gray for many a
year, but this is just downright
unacceptable. Too long have I
sailed the seas going from port to
port upwind both ways while Gray
Beard obsesses with findin' the
Great White PORCUPINE... I always
knew that ol' Gray Beard would make
a mistake sooner or later, and now
that he has, I'm here to... to...
make it right again.

                    CAPTAIN GRAY BEARD
     (v.o.)
Toothy was pleased with himself so
much he just stood there
grinnin'... that wasn't somethin'

                    CAPTAIN GRAY BEARD
          Toothy could do, on account of the
          ugliness of his toothy grin... Ugly
          or not though... He set the fires
          in motion that would ultimately
          come back to burn him.

                                        FADE OUT ENVIRONMENT

SCENE 5 THE MUTINY

                              FADE IN JOLLY FROGGER ENVIRONMENT

                    JACK
          Alright then, crew, ye should all
          know why yer here.

                                   PIRATES JEER INQUISITIVELY

                    PIRATE A
          Umm... actually we don't--

                    TOOTHY
          Of c'arse ya do! We're here ta put
          an end to this outrage!

                                              PIRATES JEER

                    PIRATE B
          Yeah, the food here's terrible!

                    TOOTHY
          Naw, naw. Listen up ya halfwits!
          We're here because a certain
          incident has proven to us that our
          beloved Cap'n Gray Beard is less
          than what a true pirate should be.
          I'm sure all of us know of plenty a
          dirty deed he's committed.

                    PIRATE A
          Why, what do ya mean?

                    TOOTHY
          I mean that all of Cap'n Gray
          Beard's crimes against all of
          piratehood are as unspeakable as...
          something... extremely...
          unspeakable! For instance, I'm sure
          y'all'f heard of the incident
          involving him and a certain gnomish
          princess.

                    PIRATE B
Yeah, and there was also the time
that he forgot 'ol Ten-Toes's
birthday.

                    PIRATE C
And I hear tell he's in cahoots
with the evil spirits! For one
time, I swear I saw him with a
maiden with a head of a snake and
the body of a red hot spike!

                    PIRATE A
And 'is tattoo ain't even real!
I've seen him wash it off!

                    TOOTHY
Ya see? These are exactly the kinda
wicked acts that are not becomin'
of a Cap'n. And I think we all know
how to resolve our problem of
havin' Gray as Cap'n, don't we?

                    PETE
Yeah, we need to steal his boots!

                    JACK
No, no! We were talking about
mutiny!

                    DRUNK PETE
Oh?... Well, that'll work, too!

                    PIRATE B
But all these crimes and misdeeds
were always overlooked until now.
Why're we really startin' this
mutiny?

DRUNK PETE
I'll tell ya why... BECAUSE!

TOOTHY
Because he has committed a crime so
intolerable that it defies all
description. So insufferable that
it's worth mutiny five times more.
So ghastly that no pirate would
dare mention the existence of such
a crime! What he's done is, indeed,
the final straw. He's the broken
the camel's back ten times over
with a single weight! He has
brought into our ranks one who no
pirate would even consider lookin'
at for the fear of bein' blinded!
One whose very presence makes a
mockery of the pirate way. I'm
speakin' of the one true misfit on
this ship. I speak of the one who
wears SILK PANTS!

.

PIRATES JEER WITH RAGE AND PASSION

JACK
And who d'ya think this silkpants
wearin' disgrace is?

PIRATE C
I know! It's him!

RUNNING SFX
STRUGGLING
PIRATE YELLS

WATER SPLASH SFX

JACK
Well, that was actually the wrong
pirate... I was referring to the
Silk-Pants... But good job anyways,
men!

PIRATES CHEER

TOOTHY
I think we've all spoken our
minds... And now we can agree that
now is the time we had a little
meetin' with the Cap'n and
introduced him to our good friend
Davy Jones... and his locker...

                    PIRATE X
But ain't that below deck?

                    TOOTHY
Yes... Very VERY below deck.

                    PIRATE X
Oh... Hurray!

                    PIRATES
Hurray!

                              GROUP RUNNING ON WOOD SFX

                    CAPTAIN GRAY BEARD
What's the meanin' of this?! Get
your hands off me, ya scurvy dog!

                    SILK PANTS
Hey! Watch the silk! Get your big
strong powerful pirate hands off
me!

                    JACK
Alright then, lads. Tie these
landlubbers up and bring 'em here!

                              CHAIN AND SHACKLE SFX

                    CAPTAIN GRAY BEARD
Jack? Pete? Toothy? OLD TEN-TOES!
What be the meanin' of this?

                    TOOTHY
I'll tell ya what the meanin' of
this be. Yer own pirates are
dead-set against ya. And have come
together in a scheming conniving
conglomeration of rebellious
reformists who have come together
mutually having the sole purpose to
insight upheaval.

                    PETE
Yeah... And to mutiny!!

                              PIRATES CHEER

                    GRAY
But... why would ye want to do
that?

                    TOOTHY
Because if they mutiny, they'll no
longer have to suffer yer foul
atrocities. They'll have a new,
stronger, more efficient leader.

                    GRAY
OH really?!...
        (beat)
Who?--

                    TOOTHY
ME, YA ID'JIT! And under me,
they'll have all the freedoms that
you so cruelly withheld from them.
I'LL let them sail wherever they
want!

                                        PIRATES CHEER

                    JACK
And kill as much as they please!

                                        PIRATES CHEER LOUDER

                    PETE
Yeah, and we're gonna steal yer
boots!

                    TOOTHY
I think the crew has spoken for
itself. We all know what we want,
and what we want is your...
Dismissal... Hee hee hee...

                    PIRATE Y
Yeah, and to kill him!

                                        PIRATES CHEER

                    JACK
So, friends, how is it that our
dear ol' Cap'n should meet his
maker?

                    PIRATE Z
Make him walk the plank!

                                        PIRATES CHEER ONE BY ONE

                    PIRATES
Walk the plank! Walk the plank!
Walk the plank!

                        PETE
SSSIIILLLEEENNNCCCE!!
     (beat)
I think we should let our NEW Cap'n
decide their fate!

                        TOOTHY
 I think our dear Cap'n should...
(screaming) WALK THE PLANK!!!

                  PIRATES CHEER
                  SWORD SFX

                                        ANGRY MOB SFX

                        JACK
Alright then, "Cap'n" Gray Beard,
have ya any last wards before we
let
yer sorry soul loose inta tha briny
deep?

                  CAPTAIN GRAY BEARD
Yes, I do!

                              FADE IN DRAMATIC MUSIC

                  CAPTAIN GRAY BEARD
I know that the devil has a special
place in hell reserved fer
mutineers. 'Tis a fate that awaits
all of ya dirty rebels fer thar
insubordination! Ya cann'a escape
it. But before yer sent ta stand,
ashamed, before yer maker, be sure
ta take heed to these last few
wards o' mine. Even though yer
souls be doomed fer-ever... If ya
have any sense in yer brains at
ALL, ye'll spare yer-selves an even
warse fate here in ye MORTAL lives
and listen to me... DON'T ANGER THE
SILK PANTS!--

                        PETE
LESS TALK MORE SPLASH!!!!!!

                  SPLASH SOUND
                                        GRAY SCREAMS

                        GRAY
(ad-lib) Help I'm drownin'- I can't
swim- I'm a pirate and I can't
swim- Ahh, I think I felt a shark

                    GRAY
bitin' me leg- Ooooohhhhhh-
Eeeeeee- Aaaaahhhhhhh-

                  DROWNING
                  SPLASHING
                                        FADE DROWNING

              SILK PANTS
No, Cap'n! Swim against the
current-- Take deeper breaths! No,
not that deep-- Oh cap'n!

              CAPTAIN GRAY BEARD
Glub, glub, glub, glub...

                    OCEAN WAVE SFX
                              FADE OUT ENVIRONMENT

SCENE 6 BACK IN THE PIRATE TAVERN

                              FADE IN TAVERN SFX

              CAPTAIN GRAY BEARD
And, well ya see, that was the last
time I saw the greatest pirate I
ever knew... Before I was washed up
here on the mainland...

              BAR WENCH
Wow, that is quite a story,
Capt'n... What do ya think happened
to the rest of yer crew?

              CAPTAIN GRAY BEARD
God only knows what the Silk-Pants
is capable of... Those scallywags
are probably at the bottom of the
sea at this point.

              SALOON DOORS OPEN
                              FOOTSTEPS ON WOOD

              JACK
Captain Gray Beard!

                              STOP TAVERN SOUND

              CAPTAIN GRAY BEARD
Well, shiver me timbers! If it
isn't those back-stabbin',
double-crossin', dirty,
good-for-nothing dogs... How the

                        CAPTAIN GRAY BEARD
hell did you escape the
Silk-Pants!?... Nevermind, don't
tell me, I'm only grateful I get to
kill ya's me self... Where's me
gun?

                                    GUN LOADING SOUNDS

                        BAR WENCH
Now, wait a minute!... We're not
gonna be having any gunfire in my
tavern...

                                    GUN COCKING SOUNDS X2
Now this here Gray Beard was
telling me a story about a
Silk-Pants pirate on the high
seas... He went on to say he was
thrown overboard in a mutiny by
what sounds like the looks of you
three... Right?

                        TOOTHY AND JACK AND PETE
Aye!...

                        BAR WENCH
Well, I ain't a fan of unfinished
stories too much, so what do you
say you three have a seat right
there next to the captain and
casually pick up right up where he
left off...

                        TOOTHY
Aww, do we have to?

                        JACK
It's so embarrassing...

                        PETE
Yeah... And none of us cried...

                        BAR WENCH
Look, you three get to finishing
the Captain's story, or I'll shoot
you where you stand for mutiny...

                        JACK
Well, when ya put it that way...

                                    CHAIRS ON WOOD SFX

                    TOOTHY
Ok but first things first...
Captain Gray Beard... You were
right about the Silk-Pants... We're
so sorry to have ever doubted you.

                    JACK
Yeah Cap'n, he beat us up real bad.

                    PETE
Yeah Cap'n! Who left that guy in
charge?!... Hey there, Sweetie,
would you mind gettin' an old
sailor a drink, thanks baby doll...

                    CAPTAIN GRAY BEARD
PETE, TOOTHY, JACK!... You are the
three most worthless pirates on the
sea... And I missed the lot of
ya... Ah, it's good to see yer ugly
faces again... So please... Regale
us... What happened aboard the
Jolly Frogger after ya's threw me
overboard?

                    JACK
Well, remember how we threw you
overboard...

                    CAPTAIN GRAY BEARD
Uh... Yes, Jack, I recall being
thrown overboard.

                    TOOTHY
Well, that's when the Silk-Pants
went nuts!

                    PETE
Yeah, that pirate's not just
pretty... He's dangerous!... Look
what he did to my shirt!

                    JACK
Wo after we threw you overboard I
turned to the rest of the crew and
I said... This is what I said... I
said to 'em this...

                              FADE OUT PIRATE TAVERN

SCENE 7 SILK-PANTS' REVENGE

                              FADE IN JOLLY FROGGER ENVIRONMENT

                    JACK
          Well that sure took care of
          him!....
                    (dusting his hands off)

                    TOOTHY
          Now then Silk arse! Yer next!!

                    SILK-PANTS
          Don't hurt me... I'm warning you...
          I'm very delicate like a flower...
          Fragile even!

                    PETE
          Well, well, well. It seems as if
          our silken princess is actually
          pleadin' fer her life!

                              PIRATES JEER AGGRESSIVELY

                    SILK-PANTS
          How dare you! I was NOT pleading!
          That was a direct order! Now that
          you've thrown Gray Beard overboard,
          I'm in charge... And I'll have you
          address me as Dutchess... Not
          Princess!

                    JACK
          I'm not sure if ya've noticed,
          SILKEY, but we're not takin' kindly
          ta arders right now.

                    TOOTHY
          It seems to me that our friend here
          has a rather loose tongue. Maybe we
          can fix that! Alright men, grab
          this filthy excuse fer a filthy
          excuse and let's take him below
          deck and introduce him to our
          favorite nifty li'l device... The
          "tongue tightener"... You two grab
          the Silk-Pants and bring him
          forward...

                    FOOTSTEPS ON WOOD X2

                              STRUGGLING

                    TOOTHY
Alright then, Silk-Pants. Do ya
have anything ta say before ya
can't say anything at all?

                    SILK-PANTS
Toothy, look, I know sometimes
things can be hard. It's okay, you
don't ALWAYS have to be so angry at
everybody. The whole world isn't
out to get you, you know.

                    DRUNK PETE
He's right, you are a little angry
sometimes...

                    TOOTHY
ENOUGH! I've heard all I can take
outta you. I'm sick a' yer singing
and yer dancing and your stinkin'
sensitivity... But most of all, I'm
sick of yer STUPID... BLOOMIN'...
SILK... PANTS!

                    CLOTHING RIP
                ALL PIRATES GASP
                    CUT OUT JOLLY FROGGER ENVIRONMENT

                    CAPTAIN GRAY BEARD
                    (v.o.)
NO!... You didn't... Tell me ya
didn't!

                    JACK
                    (v.o.)
He sure did...

                    CAPTAIN GRAY BEARD
                    (v.o.)
Why would ya go and rip the
Silk-Pants' silk pants?

                    TOOTHY
                    (v.o.)
It was the worst decision I ever
made in me miserable life...

                    BAR WENCH
                    (v.o.)
So what happened next?

                    TOOTHY
                 (v.o.)
Well that's when everything went
belly up... I turned to the crew
and I said...

                    FADE IN JOLLY FROGGER ENVIRONMENT

                    TOOTHY
Now get this sorry sod outta my
sight and tie 'im to the rack!

                              FOOTSTEPS ON WOOD X2

                    JACK
He won't budge, Captain Toothy...

                    SILK-PANTS
You... You ripped my pants.

                    TOOTHY
Enough a' yer stupid pants!

                    SILK-PANTS
You don't understand... You...
Ripped... My... PANTS!!

                    JACK
If you think anyone on this ship
cares about your silk pants, yer--

                    SILK-PANTS
YOU-RIPPED-MY-PANTS!!!

                    TOOTHY
                 (v.o.)
And that's when he went into his
dreaded pirate rage... I seen him
knock over the two pirates that
were standing on either side of
him,

                              THUD X2

and then, the Silk-Pants leaped
into the air, light as a feather,
and thrusted his sword into two
different pirates in the blink of
an eye,

                              SWORD FIGHT SFX

sending them fling off into two
different directions!

THUD X2

PIRATE MOANS

                    JACK
               (v.o.)
That's right... I remember seeing
that... Boy, he sure was deadly
with that sword...

                              SWORD FIGHT SFX

I saw him disarm one pirate while
kicking another pirate in the face,

              SWORD THUD
              FACE KICK
                                   PIRATE GROAN

and then, I saw him use another
pirate's own weapon against him to
make them die or fall overboard...
And he made it look so
effortless...

                    DRUNK PETE
               (v.o)
Yeah... And that's when he ripped
my shirt!

                    CLOTHING RIP
                  SWORD FIGHT SFX
          PIRATE FALLING OVERBOARD YELL

                                        WATER SFX

                    TOOTHY
               (v.o.)
After Pete fell overboard,
Silk-Pants continued to slash and
hack at the crew until they were
all disarmed, disabled, or dead...

                                   MUSKET FIRE

                    JACK
               (v.o.)
We tried to shoot him with our
pistols... But it was just no
use... He was much too fast for
us...

                                   MUSKET FIRE

Every shot we took at him, he
either dodged or out-maneuvered us
into some sort of whirlwind of
chaos that ended in the massacre of
many good pirates...

PIRATE DEATH CRY

                    TOOTHY
               (v.o.)
He made mincemeat out of the whole
crew until Jack an' I were the only
two pirates left...

                         SWORD FIGHTING SFX
Him and Jack had a lengthy sword
battle until he grabbed a mast-line
and sailed across the boat kicking
Jack overboard!

                    KICK SFX
          JACK YELLS AND FALLS OVERBOARD
                         WATER SPLASH SFX

                    JACK
               (v.o.)
That's right, and I remember seeing
you, Toothy, in the center of the
ship, desperately trying to load
your gun while bleeding all over
the place... I was certain you were
a goner after I was knocked
overboard... How did you ever
escape?

                    DRUNK PETE
               (v.o.)
Yeah, Toothy...? Silk-pants hated
you the most... You we're the worst
dancer...

                    TOOTHY
               (v.o.)
Well, I don't know what it was that
helped me escape with my life... It
was either by quick pirate thinking
or maybe it was vast knowledge of
sea skirmishes that kepts me from
being slain... Like Jack said, I
was loading my pistol, and I was
taking steady aim at the
Silk-pants, and then he started
walking toward me in a slow
menacing pace... I drew my gun at
the ready, but he just kept pacing
towards me... And pretty soon we
were face-ta-face and that's when I
said...

                    TOOTHY
I get it now... I get it, I
understand why they call ya... "The
DREADED Pirate SILK-PANTS!

                    SILK-PANTS
Mmmm. Isn't this nice, Toothy?
Allllll alone. Just youuuuu and
me. Mono... E... Mono!

                    TOOTHY
I never thought I'd live to see the
day I'd say this but... You win,
laddie, I'm defeated.

                                        SWORD THUD

                    SILK-PANTS
Uh-huh, tell me something I don't
know.

                    TOOTHY
I know when... I've been bested...
I couldn't defeat ya. So I
surrendered and now pirate code
says ya have to let me live and
serve on yer ship for 100 years...

                    SILK-PANTS
Uh huh, that's a nice gesture...
But... I'd rather stab ya in the
guts...!

                                        STAB WOUND SFX

                    TOOTHY
You... Really are... The most
fearsome... Most dangerous...
Dreaded... Pirate... SILK PANTS!

                            SILK-PANTS LAUGHS JOYFULLY

                    SILK-PANTS
That's right... Who's your
captain?... Captain Silk-Pants,
that's who!

                    SILK-PANTS LAUGHING
                                FADE OUT ENVIRONMENT

SCENE 8 THE PIRATE TAVERN

                    TOOTHY
And that's when I hobbled away and
dove overboard while he was
distracted laughing like a ghastly
banshee... And that was it...

                    CAPTAIN GRAY BEARD
The last anyone seen of the dreaded
pirate Silk-Pants...

                              PIRATE TREBLE WITH A CHILL
Let's lift a glass, men, and drink
to your lives for challenging the
Silk-Pants and living to tell the
tale!

                    ALL PIRATES
AYE...!

                    GLASSES CLINK

                                        SLOW CLAPPING

                    SILK-PANTS
     (slow clap)
Bravo mateys, bravo... That's a
pretty good story, only, if I would
have told it... I would have told
it better...

                    CAPTAIN GRAY BEARD
Silk-Pants!...

                                        ALL CAST GASP

Do my eyes deceive me?! Is that
you? You're alive!

                    SILK-PANTS
That's right, sailors!

                    CAPTAIN GRAY BEARD
But we thought you were lost at sea
without a crew and on a barely
seaworthy ship... How on God's blue
Earth did ya make it back?

                    SILK-PANTS
I took that little schooner of your
for a little R-and-R, and I made
port in the Orient for a bit, and
did some real soul-searching, and
lots of fur trading for fine silks

                    SILK-PANTS
and scarfs, but that got boring. So
I hoisted anchor and decided to
come back home...

                    ALL PIRATES
HOME?

                    SILK-PANTS
That's right, didn't I tell ya...
This here port is my hometown!

                    BAR WENCH
You guys mean to tell me this here
is your dreaded pirate Silk-Pants?

                    TOOTHY
Well, isn't he?

                    JACK
Yeah, isn't he?

                    DRUNK PETE
Yeah, who the hell is this guy?

                    BAR WENCH
Why, that's my brother, didn't I
tell ya?

                    SILK-PANTS
Good to be home, sis...

                    BAR WENCH
Good to have ya home, Silk-Pants.

          SILK-PANTS AND THE BAR WENCH LAUGH

                    CAPTAIN GRAY BEARD
And me ship? Where's me ship,
Silk-Pants... Don't tell me ya
scuttled her...

                    SILK-PANTS
Oh, the Jolly Frogger... She's
outside... I had her fixed up while
I was in the Orient... Added a new
paint job, too, the old color
scheme was just hideous...!

                    CAPTAIN GRAY BEARD
So does that mean I can have me ol'
ship back?

SILK-PANTS
You mean you wanna get the old gang
back together? Well ok, mateys!
Because I was working on a few new
dance numbers I think we could get
the crew to do that would just be
sen-sational overseas... And don't
think I forgot about you, Toothy,
we got a lot of work to do if we're
gonna get that timing down, what
d'ya say, men?!

CAPTAIN GRAY BEARD

I think it's the most ridiculous
thing I ever heard proposed to
group of villainous pirates... I
LOVE IT!

                    PIRATES JEER IN AGREEMENT

SILK-PANTS
Ok guys, pay attention and watch
out for the changes in the second
chorus... And a five, six, seven,
eight...

(Singing)

        ALL CAST
Oh, a sailor's life is the life for
me

How I love to sail around the
bounding sea

And I never, never, ever do a thing
about the weather

For the weather never ever does a
thing for me!

            FULL CAST LAUGHING
                    FADE OUT ENVIRONMENT

END CREDITS

                    FADE IN CLOSING CREDITS

        THE VOICE OF THE CLEVELAND RADIO PLAYERS
You have been listening to THE
JOLLY FROGGER: A one-act pirate
tale written and directed by Jack

THE VOICE OF THE CLEVELAND RADIO PLAYERS
Matuszewski, adapted by Milton
Matthew Horowitz. Starring:

Beau Reinker

Kat Bi

Charles Hargrave

Cat Kenney

Ned Kalafat

Eric Sever

Llenelle Gibson

Deanna Dionne

David Flynt

Michael Lawrence

Jack Hunt

and I'm Denny Castiglione, ladies
and gentlemen. THE JOLLY FROGGER
was recorded live in one take at
Bad Racket Recording Studio. To
purchase THE JOLLY FROGGER as an
audio book, E-book, or on 12' vinyl
please visit
ClevelandRadioPlayers.com...
scopyright 2015

Rights and Royalties

Originally adapted for the radio and performed
by The Cleveland Radio Players

Directed by Milton Matthew Horowitz

Recorded at Bad Racket Studios

For more information on performance rights and
royalties, or to listen to The Jolly Frogger as
a radio play, please visit
www.ClevelandRadioPlayers.com

www.ingramcontent.com/pod-product-compliance
Lightning Source LLC
Chambersburg PA
CBHW080812120626

46556CB00009B/3297